Mad Professor

Mad Professor

Concoct Extremely Weird Science Projects

by Mark Frauenfelder

Robot Food

Saucer Slime

Martian Volcanoes

CHRONICLE BOOKS

SAN FRANCISCO

Library of Congress Cataloging-in-Publication Data available.
ISBN 0-8118-3554-5

Designed by Ayako Akazawa
Manufactured in China

Distributed in Canada by Raincoast Books
9050 Shaughnessy Street
Vancouver, BC V6P 6E5

10 9 8 7 6 5 4 3 2 1

Chronicle Books LLC
85 Second Street
San Francisco, California 94105

www.chroniclebooks.com

Elmer's Glue-All is a registered trademark of Borden, Inc. Metamucil is a registered trademark of Procter & Gamble. Slinky is a registered trademark of James Industries.

Table of CoNtents

IntRoduction

Kia Ora is a tiny island in the South Pacific. To find it on a globe, put your finger on Hawaii and move down so that you are as far south of the equator as Hawaii is north of the equator. You'll be pointing at a country called the Cook Islands. Kia Ora is just one of the Cook Islands' hundreds of islands. It's surrounded by sparkling clear water and covered with tall palm trees, lush tropical plants, and clean white sand. Because it is so small (less than the size of a city block) and so remote (the nearest inhabited island is 150 miles away) nobody lives on Kia Ora. At least not anymore. For it has been discovered that a top-secret toy-research laboratory had, until a few years ago, recently occupied Kia Ora.

The laboratory might have remained a secret if it hadn't been for a group of marine biologists from New Zealand who went to Kia Ora to study a peculiar species of sea cucumber that lives in the shallow water off the island's shore. During the expedition, one of the researchers explored the interior of the island and stumbled on a huge crater. It was obvious that the crater had been recently formed because plants hadn't started growing in it yet. The only thing found in the crater was a purple, egg-shaped metal object the size of a washing machine.

The object was taken to the capital of the Cook Islands and presented to the nation's king. He called for his royal scientific team to examine the object.

The scientists tried to determine what the "egg" was made of. They dripped different kinds of acid on it, but the egg did not corrode. They attempted to drill it with a diamond bit, but the egg didn't show a scratch. X-rays revealed nothing. Frustrated, they banged it with a large hammer. The egg made a beautiful bell-like tone, but it didn't show even a dent.

After the scientists gave up, the king's young daughter asked if she could try to open the egg. The scientists all laughed, but the girl climbed on top and sat on it. In a moment, the egg gently swung open, revealing a thick leatherbound book titled *Zoober Science Laboratories Notebook*.

Apparently, Zoober Labs was a scientific research company that sold its inventions to toy companies around the world. The book turned out to contain a list of recipes and instructions for a variety of materials and projects. It described playful slimes and putties, miniature robots and transport devices, portable power supplies, and wonderfully strange candies. The last experiment in the book was for a working time machine.

The scientists concluded that the time machine experiment must have gone haywire. When the Zoober scientists had activated the time machine, their entire building, its occupants, and everything else within a hundred-foot radius of the time machine was sent hurtling through time; everything, that is, expect for the egg, which apparently was made out of an exotic alloy that resisted the time machine's effect.

The lab notebook was written by Zoober's four lead professors: A bald semi-invisible chemist named Philo T. Funsworth, a brilliant girl roboticist named Helena Capek, a genetically modified gorilla geologist named Tambuzi, and Professor Zoober himself, a tiny creature who seems to have come from another solar system. The professors usually referred to themselves simply as "the Zoobers."

The book you now hold in your hands contains many of the projects found in the Zoober notebook. We've selected the ones that you, as a budding mad professor, can easily complete using materials around the house. Some will require assistance from grown-ups; others you can make all by yourself. We did not include the instructions for the time machine, however. While it is surprisingly simple to build and operate the Zoober time machine (we made a working miniature out of items purchased at a convenience store), we feel that in the interest of safety, this experiment is best kept a secret.

Good luck, and have fun!

Lab Rules: Safety Notes and Lab Tips

The scientists at Zoober Labs were almost always concerned about safety. (It's too bad they didn't exercise enough caution with the time machine!) They even hired a consultant, named Safety Kid, who came to the Zoober Labs to teach them how to conduct their experiments with the utmost care. Since you, too, are going to be conducting real scientific experiments with chemicals just like the Zoobers, we've asked Safety Kid to teach you some important rules you must follow to protect yourself and ensure good results.

1. Always get a grown-up's permission before beginning an experiment. Before getting started, show this book to a grown-up and ask him or her to read the instructions for the experiment you want to conduct. Whenever you come across an experiment in the notebook with Safety Kid's picture, that means you need to be extra careful, because something hot, sharp, or potentially dangerous in some other way will be involved in the experiment. That means an adult needs to stick around while you're doing it.

2. Read the experiment all the way through before starting. That way, you'll know what you need and how long it is going to take to complete the experiment.

3. Wear safety glasses. If you think wearing goggles is for dweebs, think again. Not only do goggles protect your eyes, they make you look like a scientist, which is what you are when you conduct an experiment. While none of the chemicals and materials used here are especially toxic or dangerous, they could irritate your eyes. You can pick up an inexpensive pair of clear plastic goggles at a hardware store.

4. **Wear a laboratory coat**. Since many of the experiments use ingredients that can cause stains, you'll need to cover your clothes with a smock or other long-sleeved garment. A large, old, buttoned shirt, turned around so the buttons are in the back, works great. If you want, write your name and draw your own laboratory logo on the shirt.

5. **Set up your laboratory in an easy-to-clean area**. Many of these experiments are messy. Occasionally, little bits of goops and powders will fall out of jars while you're mixing them. Even if you promise "to be extra careful not to spill anything," you never know when an accident will happen. Before you begin conducting your experiments, you need to decide where to set up your laboratory. It's best if you can conduct your experiments in a garage or in your backyard, since people don't seem to mind as much when a beaker of gooey ooze spills on a cement floor instead of a living room carpet. A kitchen countertop could work, but remember: kitchens are used to make meals, so be prepared to close up shop right in the middle of your experiment if somebody in the house gets hungry. Remember to always clean up after you are finished, because a tidy lab ensures successful results. Always spread a bunch of newspapers on the floor to keep spills from making a mess.

6. **Do not eat your experiments**. Zoober Labs created only two or three recipes that were meant to be eaten, and those are noted clearly. Otherwise, nothing is meant to be swallowed, and some shouldn't get in your eyes or nasal passages either. While almost every ingredient used in these projects is nontoxic, some can make you sick or cause discomfort if ingested in even small quantities. Store ingredients in jars or dispose of them in the trash (not the sink) when you are finished with them, and keep out of the hands and paws of tiny kids and pets.

An Introduction to Polymer Science: Slimes, Putties, and Doughs

by Professor Philo T. Funsworth, Zoober Science Laboratories

I am Philo T. Funsworth, the world's only transparent scientist. I became transparent while trying to make an invisibility potion. The results were only partially successful. You can see through me, but you can still make out my outline. I'm the head of the polymer research department here at Zoober Science Laboratories, and I'm going to tell you a little about slimes, putties, and doughs.

The chemistry of polymers is very interesting, and making your own slimes from easily obtained materials is lots of fun, as well as a good introduction to polymer science. Best of all, making your own slime is a lot cheaper than buying it in the store.

Atoms and Molecules

All the stuff in the universe is made out of atoms. Atoms are like tiny building blocks, too small to see. There are 115 different kinds of atoms, called elements. Examples of elements include the familiar sounding ones like hydrogen, oxygen, and carbon, as well as some exotic ones like ytterbium and californium. (Ytterbium [Yb] is a lustrous silvery metal used to improve the strength of steel. It was discovered in 1878 by a Swiss scientist named Jean-Charles de Marignac. It was named after Ytterby, a village in Sweden. Californium [Cf] is thought to be formed when a star explodes violently. Scientists have been able to make californium in tiny amounts, and they sell it for $100 per 0.1 microgram. The world's richest person, Bill Gates, would have to spend his entire fortune of $40 billion just to buy less than 2 ounces of the stuff.)

Sometimes atoms like to stick to each other. Oxygen atoms, for instance, are attracted to other oxygen atoms. When one O atom (the letter "O" is shorthand for oxygen) meets up with another O, they immediately become friends and bond together. This oxygen duo is called O_2. Whenever atoms become bonded to one another, they are called *molecules*.

After the O and O atoms meet up and become the molecule O_2, they start looking for more atoms to pal around with. An O_2 pair is sometimes on the lookout for a C atom (C stands for carbon). The carbon atom is happy to link up with the O_2 molecule, and as soon as it does, the new three-atom molecule gets a new name, carbon dioxide, or CO_2.

Now that you know what a molecule is, let's study a special kind of molecule called a polymer.

Polymers–The Atom Party

Sometimes atoms decide that they want to have a party. Two or three atoms just won't do. When they feel like playing, atoms hook up in a special pattern and start forming into very long chains. These long chains are called *polymers*. *Polys* is a Greek word that means "many" and *meros* means "parts."

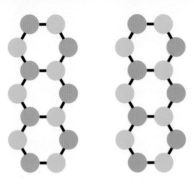

What happens when atoms form into long chains of repeating patterns? All sorts of strange stuff—they turn into glue, plastic, rubber, and many other things. Some polymers are all twisty and crinkled up. If you pull on them, they'll stretch for a long time without breaking, and then they will return to their original shape after you let go. These are a special type of polymer called *elastomers*. Rubber is an elastomer. So is slime.

How Slime Is Made

Slime is made by taking a bunch of polymer chains and adding another type of molecule that connects the chains together like rungs on a ladder. This is called cross-linking, and it makes the molecules a little harder to move around than they were before they got linked together.

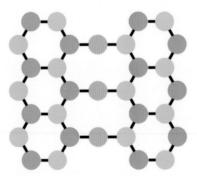

Slime at Work

Scientists are always inventing new kinds of elastomers. Many of them end up in your house—in the bottle of floor wax under the sink, in the sole of your shoe, inside your baby sister's diapers. That's right, there's a polymer powder in diapers that absorbs three hundred times its weight in liquid. This polymer was invented by scientists at the U.S. Department of Agriculture. They were looking for a way to keep water from draining away from plants. They call the stuff Super Slurper, also known as sodium polyacrylate. The same stuff is used to make "grow creatures," those little colored dinosaurs that swell up when you drop them into a glass of water. It's sometimes even used as a water supply for animals when they are transported over long distances. When the animal gets thirsty, it simply nibbles on a cube of water-soaked sodium polyacrylate that's kept along with them in the cage.

Every day, people use hundreds of different kinds of slime. We've got slime inside our body, called mucus. The mucus in your nose helps capture particles from the air you breath so they don't get stuck inside your lungs.

Did you know that some fire hoses have a powder in them that turns into slime when water is run through the hose? Firefighters like to spray a lot of water quickly to put out fires, and the powder in the hose turns into a goo that helps the water slide out faster.

This section has a bucketful of recipes to make different kinds of polymers. You'll learn how to make slimes, putties, and doughs that bounce, stretch, and wiggle. You'll even learn how to make a putty you can eat!

Goon Goo

Zoober Labs was asked by a company called Sneex Ltd. to design Goon Goo. Sneex told us Goon Goo was going to be used in the circus, but they really wanted a gooey monster with the intelligence to slither through the cracks of bank vaults and open them up from the inside. We refused to give them the Goon Goo, and Professor Zoober reported them to the police. Mr. Sneex, the owner of the company, is now in jail.

This recipe, which we have modified to prevent it from being misused, yields a playful slime with an extremely low IQ. It does not pose a threat. However, when you are finished playing with your blob of Goon Goo, don't forget to store it in a sealed container, otherwise it might attempt to escape.

Note: This stuff may stain fabrics, so be careful not to get it on clothing, furniture, carpets, or rugs.

Ingredients

2 tablespoons Elmer's Glue-All™ or other white glue
2 tablespoons water (purified water is best, but tap water is OK)
1 drop food coloring
2 teaspoons borax solution (page 16)

Tools

Glass cup
Measuring spoons
Metal or plastic spoon (for stirring)
Plastic baggie with self-closing seal

1 Combine the glue and water in the glass cup. Stir with a spoon until they are completely mixed.

2 Add the 1 drop of food coloring to the glue-water mixture. (You don't need much to tint your ooze—too many drops will give you a stain-producing blob of glop that's guaranteed to get you grounded for at least three days.)

3 Add the borax solution to the glue solution and stir. This is where the fun really begins. The mixture will immediately start to form a blob. Keep stirring. If some of the glue-water liquid does not clump together with the rest of the blob, add a little more borax solution and stir some more.

continued

4 Pour out the excess liquid, put the blob in the plastic baggie, and knead it for a while.

5 Remove the blob and play with it! This plastic polymer feels cool and clammy. It looks wet and sticky, but will snap if you pull on it quickly. It will bounce if you throw it on the ground, and slump into a puddle if you set it on a counter-top.

Hint   Add glitter after Step 1 to make "Glimmer Goo."

HOW IT WORKS: Elmer's glue contains two kinds of polymers: polyvinyl acetate and polyvinyl alcohol. The polyvinyl acetate is in the form of microscopic drops, and the polyvinyl alcohol surrounds the drops. When you use glue to stick things together, the polyvinyl alcohol dries up, which causes the polyvinyl acetate particles to clump together and become hard. When the borax solution is added to the glue-water mixture, it forms lots of rubbery "bridges" that link the polyvinyl chains. That's why you end up with a blob. This kind of chemical reaction is called "cross-linking."

BORAX SOLUTION: You'll be using the borax solution for many of the slimy experiments. To make a batch of it, just add 1 tablespoon of borax (a popular laundry additive that you can buy at most supermarkets) to 1 cup of warm water. Stir until it dissolves. Store the liquid in a jar, and label it "BORAX SOLUTION—DO NOT DRINK" so nobody will attempt to drink it!

Saucer Slime

Because we operate our laboratory in a nation comprising many small islands, we decided that the most practical means of transportation would be to use small flying saucers. Professor Helena Capek, our young roboticist, built four small but zippy saucers, and we use them to hop from island to island. They are very effective. Everybody likes the saucers, but I love them. I fly in my saucer whenever I get the chance. Sometimes I even fly a saucer while I am supposed to be working, which makes my boss, Professor Zoober, quite angry.

One of my favorite activities is dropping specially made blobs of slime out of my saucer and watching them hit the ground with a big splash. I am careful not to hit any of the animals below, and after I am finished, I land my saucer and pick up the blobs, so as not to be a litter-bug.

You can make the exact same kind of Saucer Slime that I make by following the recipe below. Like Goon Goo, Saucer Slime is clammy and jiggly, but it is clear and more rubberlike. If you don't have a flying saucer, try dropping the blobs from a tricycle or wagon, which works just as well.

Ingredients

2 tablespoons clear gel glue (but not
   Super Glue)
2 tablespoons water (purified water is
   best, but tap water is OK)
1 drop food coloring
2 teaspoons borax solution (see facing page)

Tools

Glass cup
Measuring spoons
Metal or plastic spoon (for stirring)
Plastic baggie with self-closing seal

1 Combine the glue and water in the glass cup. Stir with a spoon until they are completely mixed.

2 Add the 1 drop of food coloring to the glue-water mixture. (Remember, as with Goon Goo, too much food coloring will cause stains.)

continued

3 Add the borax solution to the glue solution and stir. The mixture will immediately start to form a blob. Keep stirring. If some of the glue-water liquid does not clump together with the rest of the blob, add a little more borax solution and stir some more.

4 Pour out the excess liquid, put the blob in the plastic baggie, and knead it for a while.

5 Remove the blob and play with it!

HOW IT WORKS: Clear gel glue is made from a slightly different polymer than white glue, so it behaves differently when mixed with the borax solution. Try mixing gel glue and white glue together with some borax solution. What happens?

Robot Food

Everything that moves needs energy to make it go. A wind-up toy uses the energy stored in its tightly wound spring. People and animals eat food, which is converted into chemical energy. Robots typically use electrical energy to keep them going, but not at Zoober Labs. The helper robots in this company consume a special substance called Robot Food. People don't like the taste, but robots can't get enough of the stuff. One thing that people and robots both agree on, though, is how fun it is to play with Robot Food. When you prod it with your finger, it seems to be wet and dry at the same time. If you grab a chunk and hold it in the palm of your hand, it will slowly turn into a shiny puddle. Try making some to see for yourself! It's safe to taste a little of it if you're brave enough. But don't get mad at us if you don't like it—we warned you.

Note: When you are finished playing with your Robot Food, either give it to a robot or throw it in the trash. Do not pour it in the sink—it might clog the pipes!

Ingredients
2 tablespoons cornstarch, or more if
   desired
Water
1 drop food coloring

Tools
Glass cup
Measuring spoons
Metal or plastic spoon (for stirring)

1 Put the cornstarch into the glass cup. Add water, a teaspoon at a time, to the cornstarch and keep stirring with a spoon. Stop adding water when it looks like pancake batter, or white school glue.

2 Add the 1 drop of food coloring and stir.

3 Play with it. Notice how it behaves when you play gently with it, and how it responds when it is handled with vigor. Observe the reaction when you squeeze a chunk tightly in your fist and then open your hand.

HOW IT WORKS: Nobody really knows why the cornstarch and water mixture acts like it does. Some think that the large starch molecules get tangled up when you add water, making them act strangely. Others think that the starch molecules get charged up with static electricity when you stir them, causing the molecules to want to stick together. What do you think?

Mister Thirsty

Be sure to have plenty of water on hand when Mister Thirsty is around! This white powder will greedily drink up to three hundred times its own weight in water, turning it into a slushy gel. Zoober Labs invented Mister Thirsty for a wealthy gentleman who is very clumsy; he spills several glasses of water every day. Now, each morning the rich man sprinkles Mister Thirsty powder on his dining room floor. As he knocks over his drinks throughout the day, the powder absorbs all the spilled liquid. By evening, the entire floor is covered in slime. He slides around in it for fun, and then takes a bath while his butler mops the floor.

There are many other uses for this super-absorbent substance. Disposable-diaper makers use Mister Thirsty in their products, garden stores sell it as a soil substitute, and toy companies use it to make "grow creatures." You can use Mister Thirsty to make a delightful slimy substance that looks like slush.

Note: Although Mr. Thirsty is shown guzzling this goo, it's certainly not meant for human consumption.

SAFETY KID SAYS: **"Sodium polyacrylate is nontoxic, but should be handled with care. Avoid getting it in your eyes and nose, too, and it needs to be thrown away in the trash, not down the sink!"**

Ingredients
1 disposable diaper, or ¼ teaspoon of "plant gel" (see sodium polyacrylate in Sources, page 76)

1 cup water (purified water is best, but tap water is OK)

1 drop food coloring

Tools
Scissors

Large plastic bag (like the kind to carry groceries)

Measuring spoons

Glass cup

Metal or plastic spoon (for stirring)

1 With the scissors, cut the disposable diaper into 2-inch-wide strips. (You can skip Steps 1 and 2 by using "plant gel.")

2 Place the diaper strips in the large plastic bag, twist the bag shut, and shake the bag for a couple of minutes. You'll see white powder come off the diaper.

3 Put about ¼ teaspoon of the powder into the glass cup.

4 Add the water and 1 drop of food coloring to the cup and stir it for about 30 seconds. The more you stir the mixture, the thicker it will become!

HOW IT WORKS: The scientific name for Mister Thirsty is sodium polyacrylate. It is both a polymer and a salt. When you add water to sodium polyacrylate, it tries to make the concentration of the salt inside and outside the molecules the same. That's why pure water is absorbed better than tap water, which contains small amounts of salt and other minerals.

Ridiculous Putty

We Zoobers were once approached by a group of private investors who were planning on building houses on Mars. Because Mars is very cold (temperatures are below freezing in the summer), the investors wanted us to make a liquid that could be shipped in vats by rocket to Mars, which they could then pour into flat molds and freeze to make windows for the houses. At first, I suggested that the investors use ordinary water to make the frozen windows, but everyone agreed that that was a boring solution. "We want you to make something fun," said the investors. So I came up with Ridiculous Putty, a funny slime that astronauts can play with on their way to Mars, and then be frozen into windows once they reach the red planet. The plan to colonize Mars was never realized, but the recipe remains.

 **SAFETY KID SAYS:** *"Polyvinyl alcohol is flammable and should be handled with care. Avoid getting it in your eyes and on your skin, and avoid inhaling it, too!"*

Ingredients

⅓ cup hot (but not skin-burning hot!) water

1½ teaspoons polyvinyl alcohol (see Sources, page 76)

3 teaspoons borax solution (page 16)

Tools

Measuring cups

Small plastic jar

Measuring spoons

Metal or plastic spoon (for stirring)

1 Put the hot (but not skin-burning hot!) water into the plastic jar. Add the polyvinyl alcohol to the water and stir it with a spoon until all the powder is dissolved. It might take several minutes.

2 Add the borax solution, 1 teaspoon at a time, stirring continually until the mixture thickens.

3 Play with it. Shape it into a ball and set it on the counter. How long does it take to turn into a puddle? Does it flatten faster if you punch it or if you press it slowly with the palm of your hand?

HOW IT WORKS: Just like in the Goon Goo and other polymer experiments, the borax solution cross-links the long molecules, making the solution thick and rubbery. Try mixing different amounts of borax solution and polyvinyl alcohol and water together to see how it affects the *viscosity* (a scientific term for how difficult it is to stir a liquid) of the Ridiculous Putty.

Nibble Dough

Nibble Dough was invented when a very nervous doll maker asked us to help him design a sculpting material that he could use to design new dolls without allowing other doll makers to steal his ideas. I came up with the idea of an edible clay, so that after the doll maker perfected a new doll design, he could eat the sculpture to prevent anyone else from finding out about it. This is the tastiest experiment in the book, so eat as much as you like—and invite your friends over to enjoy the results!

 **SAFETY KID SAYS:** *"Since this experiment requires the use of a hot oven, make sure a grown-up is around to help!"*

Ingredients
I cup butter, margarine, or shortening, at
   room temperature
I egg
I ½ cups powdered sugar
2 teaspoons vanilla extract
½ teaspoon almond extract
2 ½ cups flour

I teaspoon baking soda
I teaspoon cream of tartar
Food coloring

Tools
Baking sheet
Mixing bowls
Mixer

1 Use a tiny bit of the butter or margarine to grease the baking sheet.

2 Preheat the oven to 350 degrees Fahrenheit.

3 In a bowl, combine the butter, egg, sugar, and vanilla and almond extracts with a mixer.

4 Add the flour, baking soda, and cream of tartar. Blend well with the mixer.

5 Break the Nibble Dough into large chunks (one for each color you want), and place them into separate mixing bowls. Add a couple of drops of food coloring to each chunk and blend with the mixer.

6 Make different shapes out of the dough. Combine the colors to make rockets, bugs, robots, toys, dinosaurs, meteorites, or anything else you like. Try to keep your creations about ½ inch thick. If they are too thin, they won't bake properly.

7 Put your Nibble Dough creations on the prepared baking sheet and put the baking sheet in the oven. Bake for about 10 minutes (less for softer Nibble Dough, more for crispier Nibble Dough).

8 Take the baking sheet out of oven and let the creations cool for a few minutes before ingesting them.

No-Stick Blobs

As the chief slime scientist around here, I get requests to make all sorts of slime—oozy slime, jiggly slime, shimmering slime, glowing slime, singing slime. I have been able to make all of them—except for the singing slime, that is. So far, the best I can do is get it to hum "The Battle Hymn of the Republic." But I'm working on it! In the meantime, I have invented a bouncy, non-sticky slime that's especially fun to squeeze and pinch. I call it No-Stick Blobs.

Note: Powdered psyllium husks are available at natural-food stores as a fiber supplement.

SAFETY KID SAYS: *"Since you will be heating liquid in a microwave oven, ask a grown-up to help."*

Ingredients
I teaspoon Metamucil or powdered
   psyllium husks
I cup water
I drop food coloring

Tools
Measuring cups and spoons
Plastic jar with lid
Microwavable bowl
Metal baking sheet
Metal or plastic spoon
Knife (for cutting the slime)

1 Put the Metamucil, water, and food coloring in the plastic jar.

2 Screw the lid on and shake it for a minute or so.

3 Pour the mixture into the bowl and heat it in the microwave for I to 3 minutes, or until you see the stuff begin to boil.

4 Let it cool down in the microwave for at least 5 minutes, then heat for 1 minute longer. DON'T TOUCH IT—IT IS VERY HOT!

5 Repeat Step 4 two more times. Let sit until cool enough to handle, about 5 minutes.

6 Remove the bowl from the microwave and pour the mixture onto the baking sheet. Spread it with a spoon but don't touch until it gets cooled off, or you could get **seriously burned.**

7 Cut the cooled pieces with the knife and play with them. If you don't like the way it feels, make another batch using a little less or a little more water. Compare it to the other kinds of slimes in the book.

HOW IT WORKS: The main ingredient of Metamucil is powdered husks of the psyllium plant. Like the sodium polyacrylate in Mister Thirsty, psyllium soaks up many times its weight in water.

An Introduction to Robotics

by Professor Helena Capek, Zoober Science Laboratories

A robot is a machine that has been designed to do things that people and animals do. Some robots work in car factories, assembling and painting automobiles. Other robots mow lawns and vacuum carpets. Still others play games with people.

Robots come in all shapes and sizes. The world's tiniest robot can sit on a dime and has an onboard computer. It moves around on treads like an army tank. Its inventor says it can be equipped with a video camera, a microphone, or chemical sensors. One of the first things it will probably be used for is spying on people.

The largest robot in the world weighs 3,500 tons (as much as a million cats) and stands almost 250 feet tall (as high as a dozen two-story houses stacked on top of each other). It is designed to remove rocks from coal mines, and it can scoop up 150 tons of crushed rock at a time.

The word "robot" was invented by a Czechoslovakian author named Karel Capek. In 1921, he produced his play *R.U.R. (Rossum's Universal Robots),* which featured machines designed to look and act like people. Capek (who happens to be my great-great-grandfather) derived the word "robot" from the Czech word for boring or undesirable work, *robota*. In Capek's story, the robots revolt against the human beings and take over the planet. But there's no reason for that to happen in the real world. Humans and robots can get along well with each other, if we are patient with each other's special needs.

The Three Laws of Robotics

In 1940, another science fiction author, Isaac Asimov, introduced three laws that he thought should be programmed into all robots in order to make them safe and obedient. Here they are:

First Law:
A robot may not injure a human being or, through inaction, allow a human being to come to harm.

Second Law:
A robot must obey orders given to it by human beings except where such orders would conflict with the First Law.

Third Law:
A robot must protect its own existence as long as such protection does not conflict with the First or Second Law.

Robbie, a robot featured in Asimov's famous novel, *I, Robot,* followed the Three Laws. Robbie's owner said of his robot, "He can't help being faithful, loving, and kind. He's a machine—made so."

Many children who read Asimov's exciting science fiction stories later grew up to become robot scientists, and they tried to incorporate the Three Laws of Robotics into the robots they created.

Robots Out of Control

But in the sixty years since Asimov laid down the rules for robots, scientists have started to think in new ways about creating robots. To make smart robots that are able to adapt themselves to changing conditions, some roboticists say that we need to allow robots to evolve in the same way that life evolves on Earth. To do this, we need to stop trying so hard to control a robot's every action, and instead allow it to try new things on its own and learn from its experiences.

Of course, that means that the robots would no longer be under our complete control. We would have to watch them carefully to make sure that they don't hurt people, animals, or the environment.

As robots become more complex, the people who design them will have to think about more than motors and gears and computers. They'll have to think about how their creations will affect the world and everything in it. For example, what if you could build a robot that could make copies of itself? Would it be OK to set it free in the world? Probably not, because if the copies could in turn make their own copies, the whole world would soon be covered in robots. Or how about making a tiny flying robot that could easily devour mosquitoes? Yes, it would be great to get rid of diseases, like malaria, that mosquitoes sometimes carry, but what would happen to the birds, bats, and insects that depend on mosquitoes for food?

The robotic experiments in this book are relatively simple and just for fun. But it wouldn't hurt to start thinking about what kind of relationship we should have with robots as they become smarter and more lifelike in the years to come.

Mini Glideabout

As Zoober's robot designer, I have a special way to present my new robot creations to the other employees of Zoober Labs. I place them on tiny glideabouts that zoom through the offices. The robots are delighted to travel this way. After all, what could be more comfortable than riding on a cushion of air?

In this experiment, you'll learn how to build a miniature hovercraft just like the kind I make for my pet robots.

SAFETY KID SAYS: *"Anytime you use a glue gun, as this experiment requires, make sure a grown-up is around to help!"*

Materials

Sport-top cap from a water bottle

Unwanted LP record or CD

Large balloon

Tools

Hot-glue gun with glue cartridges (see

Sources, page 76)

1 Place the bottle cap over the hole of the LP or CD and attach it by squeezing a line (or "bead") of hot glue all the way around the perimeter of the cap. Make sure not to leave any gaps where air can escape. Remember, the glue is **very hot** and can burn your skin, so have a grown-up supervise. It will take about a minute for the glue to harden.

2 Open the sport-top spout.

continued

3 Blow up the balloon and pull the open valve end tightly over the sport-top spout. Pinch the balloon's valve, while you're attaching the balloon and until you're ready to "launch," so the air doesn't get out.

4 Set the hovercraft on a smooth floor and let it go of the balloon. Give it a gentle push to send it on its way.

HOW IT WORKS: Hovercrafts ride on a layer of pressurized air, which almost completely eliminates the friction that would ordinarily exist between the hovercraft and the ground. Large hovercrafts that carry passengers can travel over land and water at speeds of up to 80 miles per hour.

Whipmobile

Occasionally, I need to send one of my robots on an errand somewhere on the little island of Kia Ora where I and the other Zoobers work. Sometimes I need a coconut (excellent material for robot heads); other times I need pretty shells from the beach. I can't send my robots out on a hovercraft, however, because the ground is too rough. Instead, I place them on a Whipmobile, a little car that uses the springy energy of a flexible twig for power.

SAFETY KID SAYS: "This is one of the more complicated projects in the book, and it requires the use of a glue gun, so you should have a grown-up around to help!"

Materials

1 piece stiff cardboard, about 4 inches by 6 inches

Two ¼-inch-diameter wooden dowels. One should be 8 inches long and the other should be 4 inches long. You can buy dowels from any hobby or hardware store, and they will probably be happy to cut the dowels to the lengths you need.

4 large wooden spools (see Sources, page 77). Make sure the holes in the spools are larger than the diameter of the dowels so the dowels can turn freely.

2 pennies

Springy twig, about 8 to 10 inches long

2 feet strong thread or fishing line

Tools

Scissors

Hot-glue gun with glue cartridges (see Sources, page 76)

1 Cut the cardboard as shown in Figure 1. Make sure that the width of the cut-out portion (shown in Figure 1 as 2.5 inches) is wider than the length of the spool.

continued

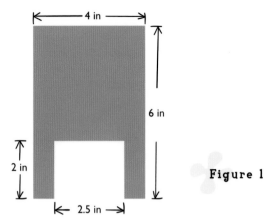

4 in

6 in

2 in

2.5 in

Figure 1

2 Center the 8-inch dowel across the width of the cardboard and hot glue it to the cardboard about 1 inch from the top edge, as shown in Figure 2. Wait a minute for the glue to harden.

3 Place 1 spool on either end of the 8-inch dowel.

Figure 2

4 Hot glue the pennies to the 8-inch dowel as shown in Figure 2. This will keep the spools from sliding off the dowel. Wait a minute for the glue to harden.

5 Place the third spool on the 4-inch dowel and hot glue the dowel to the cardboard so the dowel and spool are centered in the cut-out area, as shown in Figure 2. Wait a minute for the glue to harden.

6 Flip the cardboard over and glue the fourth spool in the middle of the cardboard, as shown in the illustration at right.

7 Stick the springy twig in the fourth spool. It should fit snugly. Tie the piece of thread or fishing line to the tip.

8 Tie the other end of the thread around the third spool (the one on the 4-inch dowel) and secure it in place with hot glue.

9 Wind up the spool so that the twig bends, set the whipmobile on the ground, and let it go. Make two or more and have a race!

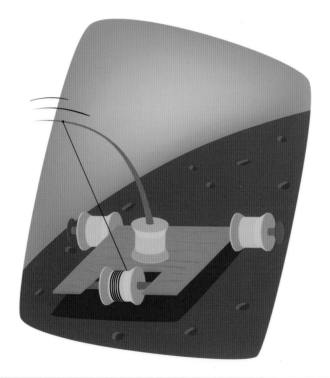

HOW IT WORKS: Just like in a real car, power from the engine (in this case, a twig) is transferred to the wheel of the Whipmobile, which propels it on its merry way.

Old Tyme Robot

This simple mechanical critter is my most beloved pet. It doesn't use electricity or even Robot Food (see page 20) to move about. It uses the power of a rubber band. I like to amuse the wild cats living on the island by placing an Old Tyme Robot in front of them and letting it crawl all around. The cats go crazy chasing after it! If you have a cat, it'll enjoy playing with the Old Tyme Robot, too.

SAFETY KID SAYS: *"Anytime you use a sharp knife, as this experiment requires, make sure a grown-up is around to help!"*

Materials

Soap or candle

Rubber band about as long as the spool

I large wooden spool (see Sources, page 77)

2 small sticks, one I inch long, the other 2 inches long, found in your backyard or nearby park

Tools

Sharp knife (any kind that can be used to carve soap or wax)

Toothpick

Tape (scotch or masking)

1 Carve the soap or candle into a disk with a small hole in the center, as shown in Figure 1. Use the toothpick to drill a hole in the disk. The hole should be slightly larger than the hole in the spool.

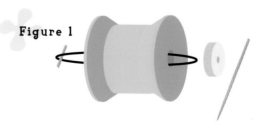

Figure 1

2 Stick the rubber band though the spool's hole and put the disk and sticks on, as shown in Figure 1 and illustration above.

3 Tape the shorter stick to the spool so it can't move. Make sure that the stick doesn't extend past the edges of the spool.

4 Wind the longer stick up until the rubber band is tight. Set it down and let it go.

HOW IT WORKS: The piece of soap or wax creates friction on the stick, which uses the energy of the rubber band to drive it across the floor. If the spool seems to be slipping, ask a grown-up to cut some notches on the edge of the spool.

Comeback Can

The Comeback Can is one of my favorite trick robots. It looks like an ordinary tin coffee can decorated with colorful paint. I like to invite people to watch as I roll the can away from me. In a few seconds the can slows down, then mysteriously returns. Everyone asks what the secret is. I tell them that the can loves me and that it gets nervous when it strays too far. But I'll let you in on the real secret: there's a rubber-band powered motor inside the can. It's easy to make.

 SAFETY KID SAYS: *"Because this experiment requires holes to be punched or drilled into a metal can, make sure a grown-up is around to help!"*

Materials
Metal coffee can with lid, or any other
    large cylindrical can with a sturdy lid
Paper clip
1 heavy nut (the kind a bolt goes in), or a
    rock the size of an egg yolk
Long rubber band
2 toothpicks

Acrylic paints
Construction paper
School glue

Tools
Drill or screwdriver
Tape
Paintbrush

1 With the drill or screwdriver, make one small hole in the center of the bottom of the coffee can, and another in the center of the lid.

2 Unbend the paper clip and twist it around the nut as shown in Figure 1. If you're using a rock, tape it to the paper clip. Then attach the paper clip to the center of the rubber band.

3 Thread the rubber band through the holes in the can and lid and stick toothpicks through the exposed loops, as shown in Figure 1. Tape them down.

4 Test the can by rolling it. If it doesn't come back to you, the rubber band might be too loose or too tight. Also, make sure the weight isn't touching the side of the can.

5 Once you're happy with the can's behavior, decorate it with paint and construction paper. Use the paper to hide the toothpicks and rubber band.

Figure 1

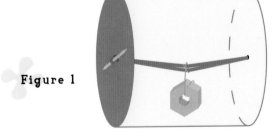

HOW IT WORKS: As you roll the can away from you, the weight causes the rubber band to wind up. This is like winding up a spring-powered toy. When the rubber band starts to unwind, the energy it releases causes the can to return to you.

An Introduction to Earth Science:
Volcanoes, Rocks, and Crystals

by Professor Tambuzi, Zoober Science Laboratories

My name is Tambuzi. I'm a genetically modified gorilla geologist with an IQ of 200. Professor Zoober rescued me as an orphaned gorilla in the mountains of Africa several years ago, and using intelligence-boosting technology developed on his planet, he made me one of the smartest beings on Earth. I chose to study geology and to make it my profession. The word "geology" comes from Greek words meaning "earth" and "discuss." Since I am a geologist, I am going to discuss the Earth with you.

The planet we live on was created about 4.7 billion years ago. Around that time, the solar system was a big swirling cloud of dust and gas. The middle part was very hot, and as the dust began to settle, our sun formed there. Smaller clouds of dust circling the sun formed into planets. One of these was the Earth.

In those early days, lots of meteorites were whizzing around, and every time one of them hit the Earth, it raised its temperature. Meanwhile, a lot of the metal in the Earth was radioactive, which made the planet even hotter. After a billion years or so, the surface of the Earth cooled down enough to form a crust. But even today, the center of the Earth is a ball of molten metal.

Volcanoes

Every once in a while the hot interior of the planet shoots through openings in the Earth's crust. These volcanic eruptions spew molten rock, hot ashes, and gases into the air, often causing a great deal of damage and loss of life. In 1985, the Nevada del Ruiz volcano in Colombia erupted, and the tide of blistering hot lava wiped out an entire city. In 1815, the eruption of Mount Tambora in Indonesia released as much energy as 6 million atom bombs.

But volcanoes aren't just destroyers; they're also creators. The Hawaiian Islands, for example, were formed over a period of millions of years as an undersea volcano sent up countless tons of lava from the floor of the ocean many miles below the surface. Hawaii still has active volcanoes, and visitors can peer into the craters and get a glimpse of the lava burbling below.

Rocks

Even though I am a gorilla, I am also a "rock hound." This is the name for a person who likes to collect rocks. I have thousands of rocks in my collection, which I store in oatmeal boxes under my bed. There are three kinds of rocks, and I have many examples of each: (1) igneous rocks, (2) sedimentary rocks, and (3) metamorphic rocks. Igneous rocks are formed from magma, which is what lava is called before it shoots out of a volcano. Some igneous rocks are hard and smooth, like obsidian, which looks like black glass. Another kind of igneous rock, called pumice, is so soft and lightweight that it can float in water. Sedimentary rocks are made from accumulated dirt and old plant and animal matter. After millions of years, this stuff hardens into rocks. Fossils are examples of sedimentary rocks. Metamorphic rocks are rocks that have changed in appearance and structure after they've been squeezed under the surface of the earth or heated by magma. A metamorphic rock called quartzite is made of sandstone that has been recrystallized by extreme pressure.

Crystals

Quartzite is a very common kind of crystallized rock, but a diamond is more popular, not just because it is rare and pretty, but because it is the hardest substance found in nature. People use diamonds to saw and drill into rocks and other hard material. The only thing that can cut a diamond is another diamond. Diamonds are made out of carbon, the same stuff that's in your pencil's "lead." But if they're both made from carbon, why is a diamond so hard while a pencil lead is so soft? The answer is that the carbon atoms in diamonds are lined up in a special repeating pattern, called a crystal structure. I know how to make many kinds of crystals, but I can't make a diamond. You need to squeeze carbon very hard to create a diamond, and even though I am a powerful gorilla, my fist just isn't strong enough! I have made crystals out of salt, sugar, and many other materials, and in my experiments, I'll teach you how to make them, too.

Subterranean Crystal Garden

When most people think of gardens, they imagine roses and tulips and daisies, with bees buzzing from flower to flower and hummingbirds sampling the different sweet nectars. But not me. I am a geologist, and I like my gardens made out of minerals. I keep several beautiful crystal gardens in my office, and I am especially pleased that they don't attract insect pests or require watering. Here's my recipe for a crystal garden that looks like freshly fallen snow on a meadow.

SAFETY KID SAYS: "This experiment requires boiling water, so make sure a grown-up is around to help!"

Materials
1 cup water
¼ cup table salt
2 teaspoons white vinegar
Rectangular sponge
Food coloring

Tools
Measuring cups
Saucepan
Metal or plastic spoon (for stirring)
Foil container, such as a disposable cake pan, large enough to hold the sponge

1 Put the water in the saucepan and bring to a boil. Remove from the heat.

2 Add the salt to the water and stir carefully (so you don't get splashed with hot water) until it is dissolved.

3 Add the white vinegar and stir. Let the mixture cool to room temperature.

4 Put the sponge in the foil container.

5 Pour the water mixture carefully onto the sponge until the sponge is soaked and there is a little extra liquid in the bottom of the container. Save any extra water mixture in a jar.

continued

6 Place the container, uncovered, where it won't be disturbed for several days. In time, crystals will begin to form.

7 Add more of the mixture to make your garden grow even bigger and more beautiful. You can also drip different food colorings on the crystals to make "blossoms."

> **HOW IT WORKS**: As the vinegar evaporates, the salt forms into crystals. Every kind of salt has its own crystal structure. For example, if you repeat the experiment using epsom salt instead of table salt, you'll see that the crystals are spiky.

EXTRA CRYSTAL FUN: Try growing one super-large salt crystal!

1 With the help of a grown-up, dissolve salt, one tablespoon at a time, into 1 cup of boiling hot water.

2 When you notice that no more salt can be dissolved, pour the clear solution into a shallow bowl.

3 As the liquid cools off, some little crystals will appear. With a pair of tweezers, gently take the biggest crystals and place them on a paper towel. These are your "seed crystals."

4 Repeat Step 1, but this time, strain the solution into a glass jar using a coffee filter or handkerchief to trap the undissolved salt.

5 Very carefully tie a thin piece of thread around the largest seed crystal and tie the other end to a pencil.

6 When the mixture is at room temperature, lay the pencil flat across the top of the jar so that the seed crystal hangs in the mixture but doesn't touch the sides or bottom of the jar.

7 Cover the top of the jar with a piece of foil to prevent evaporation.

8 Checking the jar every few days. If you are lucky, the seed will grow into a large crystal. If it doesn't work, try again with another one of your seeds. Remember, the more concentrated you make the salt solution, the larger your seed crystal will grow.

Martian Volcano

There are five different kinds of islands: barrier, continental, coral, tectonic, and volcanic. We Zoobers work on a coral island, which is made of the limestone body parts of countless tiny coral animals. I really wish that I lived on a volcanic island, but since that isn't possible, I have fun making toy volcanoes in my laboratory. Lava glows red hot everywhere, and I like to imagine this volcano is on Mars. Here's how I make it.

Materials

Bottle with a thin neck, such as a soft drink
bottle
2 tablespoons baking soda
½ cup vinegar
1 teaspoon dishwashing soap
Red food coloring
Glitter (optional)

Tools

Baking sheet or sheets of newspaper
Spoon
Measuring cups and spoons
Funnel (optional)

1 Stand the bottle on the baking sheet or layers of newspaper (to prevent spilling on the floor or table).

2 Spoon the baking soda into the bottle.

3 Mix the vinegar with the dishwashing soap and a couple drops of red food coloring. (Add some glitter if you want a sparkly volcano.) Stir gently until it's mixed well.

4 Pour the vinegar mixture into the bottle (use a funnel if that's easier) and get back.

HOW IT WORKS: When mixed together, baking soda and vinegar produce carbon dioxide (CO_2). This is the same bubbly gas in soft drinks. As the gas expands, it shoots out of the neck of the bottle like an angry volcano. (Try green food coloring for a Venusian volcano.)

Tasty Rocks

I like rocks so much that I used to try to eat them. Rocks are high in minerals, but they hurt my teeth. So I learned how to make edible rocks out of pure sugar. I eat several for dessert after every meal. (My teeth remain strong and white because I brush them frequently.) When Professor Zoober saw my gemlike crystal rock candy, he was very pleased. "We can trade the candy rocks for robot parts and other supplies!" he said. After that, we didn't need to pay for anything with money: We barter for everything we need with the candy rocks. Why don't you try making some tasty sugar rocks and see if you can buy some toys with them? That is, if you don't eat them all yourself!

SAFETY KID SAYS: "Since this experiment requires boiling water, make sure a grown-up is around to help!"

Materials

Paper clip

Thin string

Pencil

Clean, empty jam or peanut butter jar

1 cup distilled water. Note: It's important to use distilled water, since if you use tap water, the crystals might not form.

2 cups white sugar

Tools

Tape or rubber band

Plate

Saucepan

Measuring cups and spoons

Metal or plastic spoon (for stirring)

Aluminum foil (optional)

Paper

1 Tie the paper clip to one end of the string and tie the pencil to the other end of the string. Lay the pencil flat against the rim of the jar. The paper clip should hang in the center of the jar, just 1/4 inch above the bottom of the jar. Adjust the length of the string by rolling it on the pencil, then secure the string by taping it to the pencil or wrapping the pencil with a rubber band.

2 Take the pencil/clip/string out of the jar. Dip the string in distilled water, then sprinkle some sugar on it. Set it on a plate.

3 Boil the distilled water and remove it from the heat.

4 Slowly add the sugar, a tablespoon at a time, to the water and stir it carefully. You might have to heat the water on the stove some more to make the mixture clear, so there are no more sugar granules.

5 When the solution cools down a bit, pour it into the clean jar. Put the lid on it, or if you don't have the lid, use foil to cover the top. Let it set overnight.

6 The next day, take the lid off and lower the string into the jar of sugar water. Rest the pencil on the rim of the jar, so the string hangs.

7 Keep the jar where it won't be disturbed for several days. Cover the top with a piece of paper.

8 After three days, inspect the jar. Small crystals should have appeared on the string. If not, wait a few more days. If they still haven't appeared, start over, making sure everything is very clean. If crystals *have* formed, watch them grow, day by day.

9 The crystals will eventually stop growing. If you want them to get bigger, pour the sugar solution into a saucepan, heat it up, and dissolve more sugar into it. You might need to add a little water, since some of it gets lost due to evaporation.

HOW IT WORKS: At room temperature, a certain amount of water is able to dissolve a certain amount of sugar, and no more. When a jar of water contains as much dissolved sugar as it can possible hold, it is said to be fully *saturated*. If you heat the water up, it's able to dissolve more sugar. When you cool that water down to room temperature, the sugar stays dissolved in the water; this is called a *super-saturated* solution. The extra dissolved sugar is "looking" for a way to fall out of the solution, and when it finds a seed crystal (the sugar you sprinkled on the string), it attaches to that, making the seed grow larger and larger as more sugar leaves the solution.

Vortex Cannon

Did you know that volcanoes sometimes blow gigantic, perfectly formed smoke rings? Unfortunately, my volcano experiment (page 48) does not produce them. But I have a way to make them that doesn't involve volcanoes. It's called a Vortex Cannon. It will shoot a ring of smoke across the room, and it can blow out a candle several feet away. It's easy to make, and you will have loads of fun with it. Even if you don't put smoke in it, you can shoot strong puffs of air with it. Build a house of cards and shoot it down with an air blast!

SAFETY KID SAYS: "Since you need to use scissors and matches with this experiment, ask a grown-up to help."

Materials
Cylindrical oatmeal box with lid
**Big balloon, or sheet of thin rubber big
   enough to cover one end of the oatmeal
   box**
Rubber band

Tools
Scissors
Incense and matches (optional)

1 Cut a 1-inch hole in the bottom of the box. Make the hole as round and smooth as you possibly can.

2 Cut the balloon lengthwise so you end up with a large a sheet of rubber.

3 Stretch the rubber over the open end of the oatmeal box. Secure it with the rubber band.

4 Insert a lighted stick of incense into the hole, so the chamber fills with smoke. (Don't touch the balloon with the lighted end of the incense!)

5 Aim the smoke cannon at a lighted candle or other target. Pinch the balloon and release it quickly (or tap the balloon to launch a slow-moving smoke ring). You might have to practice before you start making good smoke rings.

HOW IT WORKS: When you release the pinched balloon, it quickly forces air through the hole. The air that is touching the side of the hole is slowed down by friction, while the air in the center of the hole flows freely. This creates a ring shape that rotates as it moves forward.

An Introduction to Fringe Science and the Importance of the Scientific Method

by Professor Zoober, Zoober Science Laboratories

When I left my home planet for Earth many hundreds of years ago, I brought with me a large collection of science books to read during the long voyage aboard my spaceship. In addition to the usual books about physics, chemistry, and mathematics, I also read several volumes dealing with unusual, or "fringe," science. What exactly is fringe science? It is any theory that is not accepted by the majority of scientists. You see, scientists are very cautious when it comes to accepting new ideas. They insist on checking every idea they have with carefully controlled experiments and sharing the results with other scientists so others can check their work.

The Scientific Method

When scientists perform experiments, they use something called the "scientific method," which is a four-step process for discovering how the universe operates. It goes like this:

1. Make an observation about something. (For example, observe that water freezes when it gets cold.)
2. Make a prediction based on your observation. This is called a *hypothesis*. (In our example, you might hypothesize, "Water freezes when its temperature drops to 35 degrees Fahrenheit.")
3. Conduct an experiment to test the hypothesis. (Place a glass of warm water in the freezer and stick a thermometer in it. Notice the temperature of the water when it freezes.)
4. Draw conclusions based on the results of your experiment, and change your hypothesis to match what really happened. (The water did not freeze at 35 degrees, it froze at 32 degrees!)

There's a good reason why scientists don't bother with fringe theories—most of them were not developed using the scientific method. Take the concept of perpetual motion, for instance. For hundreds of years, people have been trying to make machines that produce more energy than they consume. People have frittered away countless hours on all sorts of contraptions made out of gears, sponges, ropes, pulleys, rubber bands, pistons, gases, and magnets in a foolish attempt to generate power from nothing. Now, strictly speaking, there is no proof that a perpetual motion machine can't be made, but two hundred years of experimentation using the scientific method strongly suggests that the universe doesn't give anyone a "free lunch."

The Good Side of Fringe Science

Nevertheless, I enjoy reading about fringe science and coming up with experiments that seem a little fringy. Electric lemons? Invisible ink? Tiny flying objects? I've made them all, and more. They're fun to make, and everyone likes to watch them work.

The other reason I like to study fringe science is because once in a great while (and I do mean great), a fringe scientist turns out to be right (but only if he or she uses the scientific method to prove the discovery). Take Nicolaus Copernicus, for instance. He was an astronomer who was born in Poland in 1473. In those days, scientists were convinced that the Earth was at the center of the universe, and that it didn't move an inch. They insisted that everything else, including the other planets, the sun, and the stars, moved around the Earth. But Copernicus, using the scientific method to study the motion of the heavenly bodies, discovered that everyone else was wrong. The Earth was not at the center of the universe; it was just one of several planets in orbit around the sun. For almost two hundred years, nobody believed Copernicus except for two other scientists: Giordano Bruno in the sixteenth century and Galileo in the seventeenth century, who both proved Copernicus's theory was correct. However, it was such a radical idea that both scientists were punished by the authorities.

Luckily, in most places on Earth today, the worst thing that can happen to you for coming up with an unusual theory is that you'll get laughed at. And I must admit; some fringy ideas are quite hilarious. I never fail to be amused by you Earthlings!

Shatterproof Egg

One day, a restaurant owner visited Zoober Labs with an unusual request. It seems she had hired a breakfast chef who couldn't break an egg without dropping eggshell pieces into the pancake batter. He was an excellent chef, and his pancakes were delicious, but customers complained whenever they bit into a crunchy eggshell. The restaurant owner wanted the Zoobers to come up with a solution. I took on the assignment personally, locking myself in the research laboratory for seven and a half weeks. I emerged with a wonderful solution, which I called the Shatterproof Egg. While it didn't bounce like a ball, it was a squishy egg with a soft skin like a balloon. The restaurant owner was thrilled, and so was the chef, who added a dish to the menu in my honor, called the Zoober Frittata. What was my secret? Find out by completing the following experiment.

Note: Don't really eat the egg you make in this experiment. Because it will have been unrefrigerated for several days, it might have become inedible.

Materials
I egg
White vinegar

Tools
Drinking glass

1 Carefully place the egg in the glass.

2 Pour enough vinegar into the glass to cover the egg.

3 Set the glass where it won't be disturbed for a few days.

4 After at least three days, take the egg out and rinse it with water. Go outside or over a sink, carefully squeeze it and observe the results. What happened to the egg?

HOW IT WORKS: The egg's shell is made of calcium carbonate. This hard substance is what protects the egg. When you soak the egg in vinegar, its shell dissolves. The rubbery skin that remains on the egg is a membrane.

Sneep Bone

Aside from a large number of cats, birds, and colorful insects, the island Kia Ora doesn't have much in the way of wildlife. But during one of my daily exercise walks around the island, I came upon a strange bone poking out of the ground. To my surprise, when I picked it up, it was flexible and floppy. With a little effort, I could even tie it in a knot. I ran quickly back to the laboratory to conduct tests on it. I learned that the bone was several thousand years old, and it had belonged to a mammal about the size of a skunk. I surmised that the animal must have been a rubbery, springy animal that could bounce high enough to knock coconuts out of trees. Since I had discovered the fossil, I was entitled to give it a name. I called it a "sneep," and placed the bone in a special display case in the small museum housed in the Zoober building. The following experiment lets you make a simulated Sneep Bone out of familiar ingredients.

Materials	Tools
I cooked chicken drumstick or wishbone	Cloth
White vinegar	Drinking glass

1 Eat the meat off the drumstick or wishbone, leaving only the bone. Clean the bone with a cloth and warm water.

2 Put the bone in the glass and pour in enough vinegar to cover the bone.

3 Set the glass where it won't be disturbed.

4 After one week, replace the old vinegar with fresh vinegar.

5 After one more week, take the bone out and rinse it with water. Try twisting it and bending it. Can you tie it into a knot?

HOW IT WORKS: The vinegar dissolves the calcium in the bone, leaving the flexible cartilage behind.

Shrunken Head

The Zoobers are the world's greatest toy scientists, so naturally other toy laboratories are jealous of us. Sometimes, spies who have been hired by inferior companies sneak on the island, hoping to steal secret recipes at night while we sleep in our huts on the other side of the island. I decided that the best way to keep the crooks off the island was by scaring them away. I made a hundred realistic-looking (but phony) shrunken heads and put them on sticks planted into the ground all around the building. The next evening, some spies rowed a boat to the island and walked toward the building. The Zoobers, all sleeping in their beds, were awakened by the screams of the spies as they ran into the water. We climbed onto the roofs of our huts and watched the spies. They were so frightened they didn't even get into their boat; they simply jumped into the water and swam the whole way home. And they never returned. Here's how you can make a shrunken head just as scary.

SAFETY KID SAYS: *"Anytime you use a sharp knife, as this experiment requires, ask a grown-up to help!"*

Materials

I apple, the bigger the better

½ cup salt

4 cups water

2 tablespoons lemon juice

Acrylic paints

2 hard beans or beads (for the shrunken head's eyes)

Cotton or doll's hair

Tools

Vegetable peeler

Small sharp knife

Jar large enough to hold the apple and the water

Measuring cups and spoons

Sharpened pencils or sticks

Scotch tape or string

Paintbrush

Glue

Paper clip

1 Peel all the skin from your apple using the vegetable peeler.

2 Use the knife to carve a nose, mouth, and eyes in the apple. Ask a grown-up to carve the head for you if you are too young to handle a knife.

3 In the jar, dissolve the salt in the water. Add the lemon juice. This mixture will suck a lot of the water out of the apple. Make sure the apple will be completely covered in the solution; if not, use a smaller jar or make more mixture. Stick the sharpened pencil or stick through the top of the apple and push it deep into the core but without letting it come out the other end. Tape or tie the pencil or stick crosswise to another pencil or stick. Then tape the stick across the opening of the jar. This will keep the apple from floating to the top of the solution. The entire apple needs to remain submerged. Set it aside overnight.

continued

4 The next day, remove the head and hang it somewhere warm and dry for a couple of weeks. You can take a peek every couple of days to watch the progress.

5 When the apple is all shriveled up, take it down and paint it any color you like. Stick the beans or beads in the eyeholes if you want (although real shrunken heads don't have eyes in them).

6 Glue the cotton or doll's hair on the top of the apple.

7 When the glue and paint dry, remove the pencil. Attach the paper clip to one end of the string and poke it into the head to anchor the string. Now you can hang the head.

Top-Secret Ink

When the Zoobers need to mail a letter, we always use our special invisible ink. That way, if the letter is stolen, the only thing the thief finds in the envelope is a blank sheet of paper. I like to imagine the temper tantrums the thieves throw when they are unable to read the message. Only those who know about the invisible ink can read the Zoobers' letters, by using a secret trick that will be explained to you in the following experiment.

SAFETY KID SAYS: *"Anytime you use a sharp knife, as this experiment requires, make sure a grown-up is around to help!"*

Materials
Lemon
Paper

Tools
Cup
Small paintbrush or toothpick
Lamp

1 Cut the lemon in half and squeeze the juice into the cup.

2 Dip the paintbrush or toothpick into the juice to write the message on a piece of paper. Let the paper dry.

3 When you want to read the message, take off the shade of a lamp and hold the paper very close to the hot bulb. (Don't touch the bulb or you'll get burned!) In a few moments, the message will appear.

HOW IT WORKS: The chemicals in the lemon juice char at a lower temperature than the paper, so they turn dark before the paper does.

Pocket-Sized Rocket

I'm from a planet on the far side of the Milky Way galaxy. I made my own spaceship to come to Earth. To demonstrate my skills to the other professors at Zoober Labs, I made this tiny rocket out of a film canister. While this toy rocket isn't powerful enough to reach escape velocity and go into orbit, it might go higher than your house.

If you don't have any empty film canisters at home, ask for some at a nearby photo processing shop; these places have plenty of extras that they will usually give you for free.

Materials
Plastic 35mm film canister with cap

Acrylic paints

Construction paper (optional)

1 tablespoon vinegar

1 cotton ball

1 teaspoon baking soda

Tools
Paintbrush

Scissors (optional)

Tape (optional)

Measuring spoons

1 Decorate the film canister with paint. You can cut out a nose cone and paper fins with construction paper and tape them to the rocket if you wish.

2 GO OUTSIDE. Pour the vinegar into the film canister. Carefully push a cotton ball into the canister, making sure not to let the top of the ball get soaked.

3 Put the baking soda on top of the cotton ball, then quickly snap the cap on the film canister. Put the rocket, cap-side-down, on a flat surface and get away.

HOW IT WORKS: The baking soda and vinegar mixture produces carbon dioxide [CO_2] gas. (The cotton ball prevents them from mixing too quickly.) The gas builds up in the canister until the pressure is high enough to pop the cap off and propel the rocket into the sky.

Living Room Laser Show

After a long day inventing toys in the laboratory, the Zoobers like to entertain themselves with different tricks and stunts. One of the most popular evening events is the balloon laser show. Everyone puts a pillow on the floor and watches my colorful laser show while listening to my favorite music.

Note: You should be able to find a small mirror, about the size of a dental mirror, at most drug stores.

 *SAFETY KID SAYS: "Since this experiment requires the use of a laser pointer, be careful not to point the light directly into anyone's eyes."*

Materials
Large balloon
I sheet of cardboard
Small mirror, about the size of a quarter

Tools
Tape
Boom box or stereo with speaker
Laser pointer (see Sources, page 76)

1 Blow up the balloon and tape the tied-off end to the sheet of cardboard so the balloon stands upright.

2 Tape the small mirror near the top of the balloon, so that the reflective surface of the mirror is facing you.

3 Set the balloon on the floor and make the room dark.

4 Place a boom box or stereo speaker close to the balloon and turn on some music.

5 Aim the laser pointer at the mirror so its reflection appears on the ceiling. Make sure that you never point the laser at anyone's face, since it could damage his or her eyes.

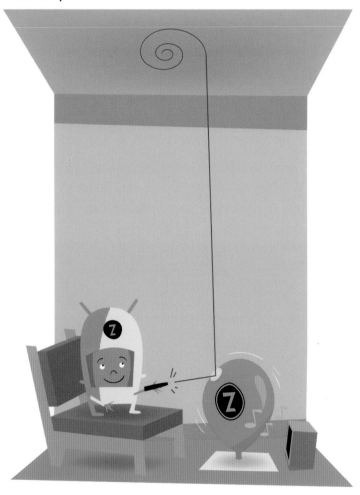

HOW IT WORKS: The patterns are caused by the sound vibrations of the music, which are transmitted to the balloon and mirror.

Milky Monkey

Everybody likes having a hobby. My hobby is making and collecting miniature plastic monkeys. I have over three million different monkeys on display in my collector's cabinet—and that doesn't count all the others I have in storage! People from all around the world come to see my collection, including kings and queens from faraway countries. Sometimes I allow visitors I've grown fond of to select a monkey from my collection to take home as a souvenir.

I use a special plastic to make my toy monkeys. It's made out of milk. I mold each monkey by hand, and then let it dry. After that, I use my paint set to decorate the monkey statuettes.

Here is my recipe for making a plastic monkey out of milk. Once you try it, you'll see why I love making them. Maybe you'll end up with a toy monkey collection even larger than mine!

SAFETY KID SAYS: *"Since this experiment requires you to boil liquid on the stove, make sure a grown-up is around to help!"*

Ingredients
⅔ cup milk (any kind, skim, lowfat, or
  whole will do)
3 teaspoons white vinegar

Tools
Measuring cups and spoons
Saucepan
Metal or plastic spoon
Glass jar
Acrylic paints and brush

1 Pour the milk into the saucepan. Add 2 teaspoons of the white vinegar. Heat the mixture until it begins to boil, then turn off the stove. Soon, little globs will start to form. The liquid will begin to turn clear.

2 Pour the clear liquid out of the saucepan and down the drain. Using a spoon, put the globs into the jar.

3 Add the remaining 1 teaspoon of vinegar to the glass jar and stir. Leave the stuff alone for a couple of hours.

4 Remove the globs and wash them in water. Pour the remaining liquid down the drain.

5 Knead the globs together until they form a ball and have the consistency of clay. Mold a monkey out of it. (Or, mold any another animal, such as a prairie dog or caterpillar.) Let the monkey dry for at least 24 hours.

6 Paint and enjoy your creation!

HOW IT WORKS: The combination of vinegar and high temperature separates milk into curds (the globs) and whey (the liquid). The curds contain fat, minerals, and a plastic-like protein called *casein*. Casein molecules are very long and stretchy, making them easy to mold.

Fruity Power Plant

We Zoobers need a lot of electricity to run our company, but no energy company is willing to string power cables all the way over to our island. But I noticed that the island is full of lemon trees. I knew that I could make batteries from the lemons, and I went to work constructing a power plant using tens of thousands of lemons for electricity. Besides providing us with all our energy requirements, the entire building smells lemony fresh. The following experiment shows you how to build a miniature lemon power plant that can illuminate a lightbulb.

Note: You can buy the copper wire and lightbulb at most hardware or hobby stores.

 **SAFETY KID SAYS:** *"Since you need to use a knife and wire strippers with this experiment, ask a grown-up to help."*

Materials
4 to 5 feet insulated copper wire

6 to 8 paper clips

6 to 8 lemons

Tiny lightbulb with screw contacts

Tools
Wire strippers

Knife

1 Use the wire strippers to cut the wire into 6-inch pieces. If you have 6 lemons, you need 7 wires. If you have 8 lemons, you need 9 wires.

2 Strip about an inch of the plastic insulation from both ends of each wire.

3 Straighten one end of each paper clip and wrap a wire around each hooked end, as shown in the illustration.

4 Stick the paper clips and wires into the lemons as shown in the illustration. Connect the last 2 wires to the screw contacts of the lightbulb.

5 If the lightbulb doesn't shine, that means it is not getting enough electricity. You might need more lemons. You can also cut the lemons in half to double the strength. If that fails, try using a smaller lightbulb.

HOW IT WORKS: Electricity is produced when tiny particles called electrons move from one place to another. The lemon's acidic juice can carry the electrons existing in the copper wire over to the iron paper clips.

Reverb-O-Phones

I'm not the only alien scientist living on your planet. In fact, there are six of us on Earth, and we are in constant communication. For example, my colleague, Professor Toober, lives near the Batu Caves in Malaysia. When we need to speak to one another, we use our special Reverb-O-Phones. These are similar to the toy phones you can make with paper cups and string, except we add a piece of coat hanger between the cups. The coat hanger gives our voices an echo-ey, metallic sound. It may sound strange to you, but because our ears are different from human ears, we prefer it. Try making some Reverb-O-Phones and see how you like it.

SAFETY KID SAYS: *"Since you need to use wire cutters with this experiment, ask a grown-up to help."*

Materials
2 paper cups
One 20- to 30-foot-long piece of string
   (kite string is good)
2 paper clips
Metal coat hanger

Tools
Pencil
Wire cutters
Scissors

1 Use the pencil to punch a small hole in the bottom of each cup.

2 Put one end of the string through the bottom of each cup from the outside, so the end is inside the cup.

3 Tie a paper clip to each end of the string, to keep the string from coming out of the cups.

4 Use the wire cutters to snip the twisted top off of the coat hanger, as shown in the illustration at right.

5 Cut the string in half and tie the coat hanger to each side of the hanger, as shown in the illustration below.

6 Find a friend to play with you. Stretch the cups tightly and takes turns talking and listening. If you round up a third friend, have him or her bonk on the coat hanger with a pencil while you listen in the cup.

HOW IT WORKS: Sound waves travel differently through different materials. You are familiar with hearing sounds as they travel through the air. When sound travels through string and metal, certain frequencies are filtered out, making your voice sound weird. For different sounds, try substituting other objects in place of the coat hanger, such as a spring from a ballpoint pen or a Slinky toy.

Portal Paper

Even though I'm under two and a half feet tall, people still doubt me when I tell them I can walk through a hole cut out of standard 8½-by-11-inch sheet of paper. When I explain that anyone, regardless of height, can walk through the hole, they tell me that I'm crazy. Well, I may be crazy, but that doesn't make me a liar. Here's how I do it.

Materials
1 sheet of 8½-by-11-inch typing paper

Tools
Scissors

1 Look at the illustration. Notice that the paper I'm holding has dotted lines. Use the scissors to cut out the same pattern in your piece of paper. You may need to make more cuts in your paper than you see in my paper. (I'm probably a lot smaller than you).

2 Carefully open the big zigzag hole you've just cut and step through it.

HOW IT WORKS: By making the back-and-forth cuts in the paper, you are increasing the length of the edges of the paper, even though the total area remains the same. In theory, you could cut a hole in a piece of paper big enough for the Earth to go through.

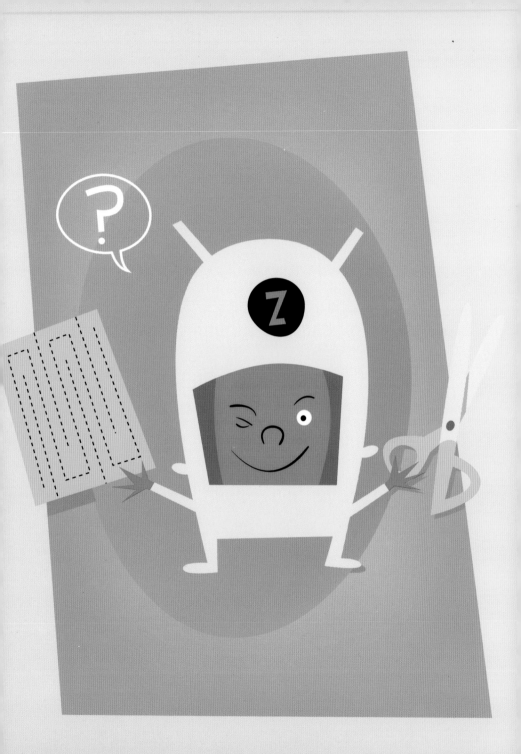

SoURces

Everything you need to conduct most of the experiments in this book can be found at any supermarket or hardware store. A few experiments require special chemicals or materials. Here is a list of sources:

Sodium polyacrylate (used in Mister Thirsty, page 22). The easiest way to obtain sodium polyacrylate is by cutting open a fresh disposable diaper. If you want large amounts of the stuff, you can order it online from www.plantgel.com. It costs $5 for a package that will make one gallon of gel. You can get a free sample by sending a self-addressed, stamped envelope to:
>DNB Designs
>4164 Austin Bluffs Pkwy, # 207
>Colorado Springs, CO 80918

Polyvinyl alcohol (used in Ridiculous Putty, page 24). Polyvinyl alcohol is a white powder that dissolves in warm water. It is one of the main ingredients in store-bought toy slime. You can buy it at most scientific supply stores. Tri-Ess Sciences, Inc. (www.tri-esssciences.com) sells polyvinyl alcohol. You can order it from their Web site, or by calling 800-274-6910 (outside California) or 818-848-7838 (inside California). The Chemistry Store also sells polyvinyl alcohol, go to www.chemistrystore.com/Polyvinyl_alcohol.htm. Both Tri-Ess and the Chemistry Store are good places to buy jars, mixing spoons, and other laboratory glassware.

Hot-glue gun. Several experiments call for a hot-glue gun. Most hobby and hardware stores sell them for under $5, and they usually come with a couple of glue sticks. Amazon.com's "Tools and Hardware" store sells a variety of glue guns, with prices starting at $4.99 for a mini glue gun (perfect for the projects you are going to work on in this book). Just visit Amazon.com's Web site and search for "glue gun." Remember, the glue that comes out of these guns is **very hot** and can cause **severe burns** if it comes in contact with your skin. Please use them under adult supervision only.

Wooden spools (used in Old Tyme Robot, page 38, and Whipmobile, page 35). Unfortunately, most sewing thread today comes on plastic, not wooden, spools. You might be able to find some wooden spools at a hobby shop, or you can order a bag of sixty wooden spools in various sizes for $8.95 from tuffware.com/arts-crafts/crafts/spools.html. You can also buy "old-fashioned" wooden spools (which work very well for these experiments) for 30¢ each from www.rbdesigns.com/howee/spools.html.

Laser Pointer (used in Living Room Laser Show, page 66). Amazon.com sells twenty different kinds of laser pointers for as little at $4.99. Search for "laser pointers."

For FuRther ExpLorAtion

Hopefully, this book has whetted your appetite for more science. Here's a list of books, museums, and Web sites that I especially like.

BOOKS

The New Way Things Work by David Macaulay. This wonderful book uses humorous illustrations to clearly explain the inner workings of the machines that surround us.

Chemical Chaos by Nick Arnold and Tony De Saulles. Did you know that one of the most important ingredients in modern ice cream is seaweed? Do you know what makes a stink bomb smell so bad? You'll find out after reading this disgustingly terrific book, part of the "Horrible Science" series.

MUSEUMS

The Exploratorium (3601 Lyon Street, San Francisco, CA 94123, 415-EXP-LORE). Any big city worth its sodium chloride has a science museum, but for those interested in rolling up their sleeves and conducting real experiments, the Exploratorium is a great place to spend a day (or two). With dozens of hands-on experiments that demonstrate physics, chemistry, optics, biology, and electronics, this giant museum will keep visitors of all ages busily fascinated.

A huge list of science museums is available on Yahoo! at dir.yahoo.com/Science/Museums_and_Exhibits/.

WEB SITES

Cool Science for Curious Kids (www.hhmi.org/coolscience/). Learn about the strange world of dust particles and how to classify animals at this great biology site for kids.

The Comic Book Periodic Table of the Elements
(www.uky.edu/Projects/Chemcomics/). Find out which comic book characters are associated with different chemicals by clicking on the elements of the periodic table. Look over there—it's Rubidium Man!

Acknowledgments

Writing and illustrating this book was a lot of fun. The support and comments of my family and friends made it even more fun. I'd like to thank the following people for their helpful suggestions and ideas:

David Pescovitz, Kelly Sparks, Gareth Branwyn, Cory Doctorow, Douglas Rushkoff, Susan Sheridan, Jim Leftwich, Marc Weingarten, Wendy Frauenfelder, Alberta Chu, Kevin Kelly, Jenn Shreve, Carl Schaefer, Craig Shapiro, and Elizabeth Kruger looked at my drawings and experiments and gave me great advice.

My father, Lew, is a garage scientist of the highest order, and built a lot of neat toys for me when I was a kid, including a miniature radio transmitter and a digital wristwatch, back when people had never even heard of them. He was, and still is, a great inspiration, as is my mother, Nina, who never became *too* upset when I made a mistake, such as setting my neighbor's kitchen on fire while making smoke bombs or filling the house with thick black smoke while making fingerprint powder.

I wish to thank my editor, Alan Rapp, who worked with me for months to develop the book's concept. His gentle support and creative ideas were the perfect launching pad for this book. Thanks also to my copy editor, Jeff Campbell, and designer, Ayako Akazawa, for their great work.

Finally, I want to thank the two most important contributors: my wife, Carla, who gave me all sorts of terrific ideas for the drawings, and my daughter, Sarina, who eagerly tested the experiments and provided honest feedback as only a four-year-old can.

Thank you all!

ZOOBER TOY LAB

YOURS IN SCIENCE,
PROF. ZOOBER